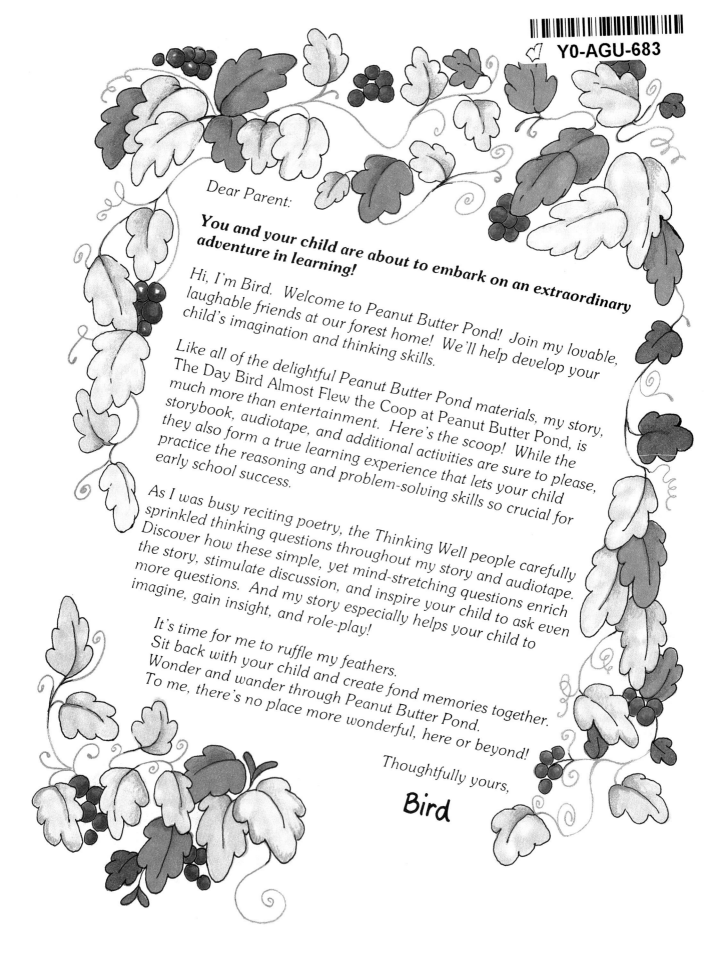

Dear Parent:

You and your child are about to embark on an extraordinary adventure in learning!

Hi, I'm Bird. Welcome to Peanut Butter Pond! Join my lovable, laughable friends at our forest home! We'll help develop your child's imagination and thinking skills.

Like all of the delightful Peanut Butter Pond materials, my story, The Day Bird Almost Flew the Coop at Peanut Butter Pond, is much more than entertainment. Here's the scoop! While the storybook, audiotape, and additional activities are sure to please, they also form a true learning experience that lets your child practice the reasoning and problem-solving skills so crucial for early school success.

As I was busy reciting poetry, the Thinking Well people carefully sprinkled thinking questions throughout my story and audiotape. Discover how these simple, yet mind-stretching questions enrich the story, stimulate discussion, and inspire your child to ask even more questions. And my story especially helps your child to imagine, gain insight, and role-play!

It's time for me to ruffle my feathers.
Sit back with your child and create fond memories together.
Wonder and wander through Peanut Butter Pond.
To me, there's no place more wonderful, here or beyond!

Thoughtfully yours,

Bird

A division of LinguiSystems, Inc.

Other products in the Peanut Butter Pond Series:

Thinking Well
3100 4th Avenue
East Moline, IL 61244

1-800-U-2-THINK

The Day Bird Almost Flew the Coop

at Peanut Butter Pond

Story by Lael Littke

Illustrated by Stephanie McFetridge Britt

One morning, Bird came out of his house in Tall Tree and looked around. Golden sunlight sparkled on Peanut Butter Pond. A south wind whispered through the green forest. The sky was bright blue.

"Nature's art adds soft adorning
 To this lovely early morning," Bird said.

He ruffled his feathers, thrilled with his own words.

Why does Bird like living in Peanut Butter Pond?

Bird chirped,
"Since I'm such a first-rate poet,
People everywhere should know it.

I truly think it is a pity
That I don't live in a city."

The more Bird thought about it, the more he liked the idea of living in a city where thousands of people could hear his poetry.

Bird declared,
  "And so,
    I'll go!"

Why does Bird want to go to the city?

Bird fluttered down to tell Beaver his plan. Beaver was sunning himself on
the wooden deck he'd built on top of his dam.

Bird told Beaver,
    "I'll go away this very day.
      I'll pack my things, then flap my wings."

"Go away?" Beaver looked startled. "Why?"

Bird spread his wings and replied,
    "To be a poet. I guarantee
        Someday you will hear of me."

He flew up to his house in Tall Tree to pack.

"We've already heard of you, Bird," Beaver called after him.

But Bird scarcely heard a word.

Why didn't Bird hear what Beaver said to him?

When Bird came back out of his house with his suitcase, he saw that Beaver had gathered all the Peanut Butter Pond critters together. Snake was there, and Skunk and Woodchuck and Porcupine and Possum. Possum's five children were there, too.

"I'm having a party for you, Bird," Beaver said. "Everybody wanted to get together to say good-bye to you."

Bird was pleased.

BARK BARBQ

BUG BUNS

BLUEBERRY BUCKLE

Why are they having a party if their friend is going away?

Bird fluttered down to Beaver's dam and said,
  "I'll stay. Because I'm going by wing,
    There are no trains to catch or anything."

Bird and his friends talked and laughed and ate the bark barbecue and bug buns and blueberry buckle Beaver had prepared.

What do you think bark barbecue tastes like?

Then everybody went swimming in Peanut Butter Pond.

The animals had so much fun at Bird's going-away party that it was dark before they all went home.

Bird said wearily,
    "It's hard for me to see at night.
    I'll fly tomorrow when it's light."

Why didn't Bird leave for the city right after the party?

The next morning Possum said, "You can't just leave today without a proper send-off, Bird. I'll get everybody together, and we'll have a picnic while we say good-bye."

Possum fixed pickled polliwogs, popcorn patties, and parsley pastry for the picnic.

What foods would you serve at a going-away picnic for Bird?

Everyone came to Bird's going-away picnic. They ate on the banks of Peanut Butter Pond. They played Ring Around the Birdie and London Birdie's Falling Down with Possum's children.

How are the games they played like games you play?

After the picnic, Bird flew up to his house in Tall Tree and sang
a farewell song.

Snake wiped away a tear with the tip of his tail as he listened. "I ssssimply
can't sssstand to ssssee you go, Bird, without having a ssssspecial dinner in
your honor. If you'll wait just one more day, I'll fix sssssizzling sssslug
sssssoufflé, sssssnail sssssandwiches, and sssssparkling sssssassafrass sssssoda."

Bird could feel his mouth water. He said,
        "One day?
         I'll stay!"

The next day all the animals came to Snake's fancy dinner, served on top of a log under Tall Tree.

Everybody ate. Then Snake showed them how to do snake dances.

Why is it so easy for Snake to do snake dances?

At the end of the day, Bird rubbed his full craw with his wing.
"If I get any fatter,
I'll fall and I'll splatter
When I try to fly.
So now it's good-bye."

"Oh, no," the animals groaned.

"Peanut Butter Pond won't be the same without you here, Bird," Skunk said.

Porcupine looked very unhappy. "I wish you didn't have to go."

What other things could the animals do to show Bird they will miss him?

"Exactly why are you going to the city, Bird?" Woodchuck asked.

Bird ruffled his wings and chirped,
"To say my rhymes
And have good times
And live a poet's life.
To live in a tree and . . ."

Why is Bird going to the city?

"But, Bird," objected Woodchuck, "you live in a tree here. And you say your rhymes and certainly have good times."

Bird nodded.
   "That's true, of course, but in the cities,
      There are many more people to hear my ditties."

"There are many more poets, too," Woodchuck said.

Bird thought about what Woodchuck had told him. In the city, there was probably a poet in every tree. Would anyone want to listen to him?

At Peanut Butter Pond, he was the one and only poet.

Why are there so many poets living in the city?

"It would be sad to be unheeded.
I'd better stay where I am needed," Bird decided.

"Hurray!" yelled Snake and Skunk and Woodchuck and Beaver and
Porcupine and Possum. "Hurray!" yelled all five of Possum's children.

Woodchuck climbed up on a stump where he could be heard. "Everybody come to my den," he said. "We'll have a welcome–home party for Bird."

How is a welcome-home party different from a going-away party? How are they alike?

Everyone came to Bird's welcome–home party. Woodchuck fixed worm wieners, weevil waffles, and watercress wafers for refreshments.

They all had such a good time that Skunk said, "I'll have a welcome–home breakfast for everybody tomorrow."

Bird smiled happily and said,
   "There's no place in the world beyond
   As nice as Peanut Butter Pond."

Poetry
BY BIRD

Think 'n' Tell

If you gave Bird a going–away present, what would you give him? Why?

How would Peanut Butter Pond be different without Bird?

How are Peanut Butter Pond and a city different? How are they alike?

How would Bird's friends feel if he had moved away without telling them why he was leaving?

Do you think Bird will ever move to the city? Why?

Bird's Nest

Bird sleeps in a wooden house at Peanut Butter Pond, but when he visits his friends in the city, Bird sleeps in a nest made from grass and twigs. Build a nest made from grass and twigs. Then, invite Bird to spend the night at your house.

What you need:

brown and blue Play-Doh
grass
twigs

What to do:

1. Shape the brown Play-Doh into a nest.

2. Press some grass and twigs into the nest.

3. Shape some blue Play-Doh to make Bird.

4. Put Bird in his nest.

Goodnight.
Sleep tight!

Would Bird rather sleep in a birdhouse or in a nest? Why?

Bug Bun

All of the animals at Peanut Butter Pond love Beaver's bug buns. So, Beaver served them at Bird's going-away party. Maybe your family will love bug buns, too. Make one large, delicious bug bun for your family's dinner tonight.

What you need:

refrigerator biscuit dough
cookie sheet
pretzel sticks
raisins

What to do:

1. Put six biscuits on a cookie sheet end to end.

2. Push one pretzel into each side of each biscuit to make legs.

3. Push two raisins into the first biscuit to make bug eyes.

4. Push two pretzels into the first biscuit to make antennas.

5. Bake at 325 degrees until your bug bun is a crispy golden brown.

Or, create your own special bug bun using chow mein noodles, peanuts, icing, etc.

Why would Peanut Butter Pond animals like bug buns?

A Spoon and Fork Bird

Bird saved the plastic spoons and forks from his going-away parties. He used them to make spoon and fork birds for all his Peanut Butter Pond friends. Save your plastic spoons and forks and make your own birds. Don't let them fly too far from home!

What you need: plastic spoon and fork
glue
construction paper

What to do:

1. Glue the handles of a plastic spoon and fork together. The bowl of the spoon is the head, and the fork is the tail feathers.

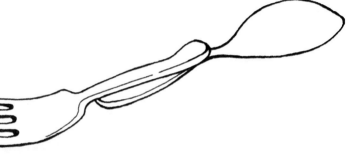

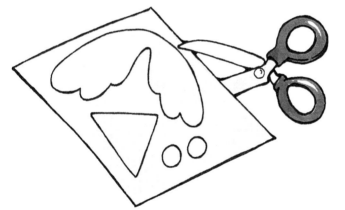

2. Draw, then cut out a one-piece pair of paper wings, a beak, and eyes from the construction paper.

3. Glue the wings across the handles. Glue the beak and eyes to the spoon.

If your spoon and fork bird could fly, where would he go? Why?

Bird, Please Don't Fly Away